The
Apartment House
on Poppy Hill

By **Nina LaCour**

Illustrated by **Sònia Albert**

chronicle books · san francisco

For Juliet —N. L.

Library of Congress Cataloging-in-Publication Data

Names: LaCour, Nina, author. | Albert, Sònia, illustrator.

Title: The apartment house on Poppy Hill / by Nina LaCour ;
illustrated by Sònia Albert.

Description: San Francisco : Chronicle Books, [2023] | Series: The
apartment house on Poppy Hill ; book 1 | Audience: Ages 7-10.

Identifiers: LCCN 2023005996 | ISBN 9781797213736 (hardcover)

Subjects: LCSH: Apartment houses—Juvenile fiction. | Apartment
dwellers—Juvenile fiction. | Neighbors—Juvenile fiction. |
Interpersonal relations—Juvenile fiction. | CYAC: Apartment
houses—Fiction. | Neighbors—Fiction. | Interpersonal
relations—Fiction. | Mystery and detective stories. | LCGFT: Detective
and mystery fiction. | Humorous fiction.

Classification: LCC PZ7.L13577 Ap 2024 | DDC 813.6 [Fic]—dc23/eng/20230214

LC record available at https://lccn.loc.gov/2023005996

Manufactured in China.

Design by Jennifer Tolo Pierce.

Typeset in Albra, Grenale, and Bourton.

10 9 8 7 6 5 4 3 2 1

Chronicle Books LLC

680 Second Street

San Francisco, California 94107

Chronicle Books—we see things differently. Become part of
our community at www.chroniclekids.com.

WELCOME, FRIEND.

This is no ordinary apartment
house, but you are no ordinary visitor.

Before you enter,
here's what you should know:

Calamities befall,
tires flatten, plans change, a day passes
and you barely know it.

A rose can be a flower or a girl or a tiny gold pin.

Time is everything and nothing
and something in between.
What matters is that you pay attention.

All right now, enough of that.
Come right in and take off your shoes.

our best regards,
the Robinsons

New Neighbors

CHAPTER ONE

1106 Wildflower Place was what many considered to be a perfect building, plunked right in the middle of Poppy Hill, a not entirely perfect hill but a good one all the same.

The building wasn't at the top of the hill, and it wasn't at the bottom. Its pink paint was neither too bright nor too pale. Its trim was green like a forest, with metallic gold stars. Even when fog settled over the rest of the city—as the San Francisco fog was known to do—the sun still shone warmly across Poppy Hill.

And it shone especially bright through the windows of 1106 Wildflower Place, Apartments A through E.

Ella Josephine Norwood would know. She had lived on the middle floor, in Apartment C, ever since she was born.

On this day, Ella was watching the newest tenants pull up out front in a moving truck. She waved her arms out her window to get their attention.

"Just angle your tires to the curb!" she called down on their seventh attempt to park on the tremendously steep street. "And don't worry!" she added. "I've lived here my whole life. Nine *entire* years. I'm coming down to help!"

The new tenants' names were Leo and Cleo, and they were moving into Apartment E, which was on the ground floor.

"There are things you should know about your new residence," Ella told them as they carried a fuzzy orange sofa up the front steps, into the shared entry hall, and through the door of Apartment E. "There's a trick with your oven and a glitch with your light switches. And then there are the garden rules, of course. I'm sorry to tell you, but they are very strict."

"Excuse us," Leo said. "You're blocking the door."

"You should also know about a sound at night that's a little . . . *alarming* at first," Ella said, stepping aside and then following them back to the truck. "You'll get used to it, but be prepared."

"Maybe later," Cleo said in a very sweet voice.

A too-*sweet voice*, Ella thought.

"Okay?" Cleo asked, and smiled. She was carrying a box marked HEAVY.

"Okay," Ella said, and smiled back.

Cleo smiled wider.

Ella smiled wider, too.

"Um, excuse me?" Cleo said, tilting her head. Her smile got *so* wide it looked a little painful.

"Oh, sure," Ella said. "You are excused." She didn't know what, exactly, Cleo needed excusing for, but she was always happy to help.

Well, almost always, anyway.

"Um . . . you're blocking the door again?" Cleo said.

"Oh!" Ella laughed. "Okay, okay, I know when I'm not wanted."

She began the stomp up the stairs to Apartment C.

Before shutting her door, she called down, "I'll be right on top of your heads if you need me!"

CHAPTER TWO

"They didn't take me up on *any* of my offers!" Ella told her mother, Abby, hours later.

Ella was supposed to be peeling carrots, but she had trouble focusing on talking and peeling at the same time.

And Ella had been talking since dinner prep began.

Abby had preheated the oven. She'd chopped broccoli and slid the baking sheet onto the top rack. She'd rinsed the lettuce and sliced the radishes. She'd made salad dressing. She'd heated the oil in the pan and breaded the fish.

And in the time it took for Abby to do all that, Ella had peeled precisely one half of a single carrot.

"I mean *really*," Ella was saying now. "I've lived here my entire life. I have so much useful information for them! And they didn't want to hear any of it!"

Livy, her other mother, appeared in the doorway.

"Is this about the new neighbors?" Livy asked. Her clothes were covered in paint, as always. Her hands were full of paintbrushes, as always. As always, a smear or two of paint was in her hair.

"Yes!" Ella said. "They are impossible."

"Impossible how?" Livy asked, crossing to the sink.

"Well, first they were so nervous about parking the truck. *It's just a steep hill, people! Get used to it!*

You live here now! And then they had this sofa that is *fuzzy* and *orange!* And they are so young, they are *barely* grown-ups."

"Ella," Abby said.

But Ella didn't hear her. "Seriously," Ella went on. "Are they even old enough to have their own apartment?"

"That will be nice, to have a young couple in the building," Livy said as she rinsed her paintbrushes.

Abby tried again. "Ella?"

"And I started to tell them about the things that I know—things that they should definitely hear about—but they didn't want to listen!"

"Ella!" Abby said. "You're walking in circles."

Ella stopped. It was true. She had been walking in circles around the kitchen island. She had been walking in circle after circle with a carrot in one hand and a peeler in the other. She had forgotten about peeling the carrots entirely.

"Here," Abby said. "Hand them over."

Ella handed her the carrot and the peeler.

Livy said, "Come along with me. Let it all out."

Ella followed Livy into the living-room-slash-dining-room-slash-painting-room-slash-office and told her the rest while Livy screwed the lids back onto her paints and cleared off the table. Usually, Ella would help with the napkins and silverware, but she was too worked up.

"The smile on that lady! I mean, if I'm in your way, just tell me! If I'm in your way, don't say 'excuse me' when you really want *me* to excuse *myself*! That's just confusing!"

"That does sound confusing," Livy said as she lit a candle at the center of the table. "It sounds very, very confusing."

"Ugh!" Ella said. She stomped her right foot. "Ugh!" she said louder. She stomped her left foot. "UGH!" She stomped both feet at once.

"All done?" Abby asked, carrying the dinner plates into the room.

"Yes," Ella said.

"Great," Abby said. "Let's eat."

CHAPTER THREE

Leo and Cleo heard a *thump*, followed by a second *thump*, followed by a loud third *thump*.

"Is this an earthquake?" Leo asked, dashing out of the kitchen.

"I don't think so," Cleo said. She was sitting on the orange sofa, which they'd placed under the window. She'd been staring at the towers of boxes, wondering where to start, when the thumps had begun. "I think," she said, "that the sound is coming from on top of our heads. But it appears to be over now."

Cleo wore a thin gold engagement band on the ring finger of her left hand. In the middle of it was a tiny diamond. She liked to watch it sparkle.

"Look," she said now. "My ring is casting dots of light onto the ceiling."

Leo followed Cleo's gaze at the specks of light. They were very pretty. He looked at Cleo.

"Here we are," he said. "In our very first place."

"Isn't it perfect?" Cleo said.

"It is," he said. "It's just . . . I can't seem to get the oven to work."

"Hmm," Cleo said. "Well, let's go have a look."

CHAPTER FOUR

An hour later came a knock on the door of Apartment C. It was a soft, rather sheepish knock. It was a knock that sounded sorry to even be knocking at all.

Livy and Abby opened the door. There, on the other side, were Leo and Cleo.

"You *are* young," Livy said.

"I hope the cooking odors weren't too strong," Abby said. "Fish can really stink up the place."

"Your dinner smelled great," Leo said. "Not stinky at all. But speaking of dinner . . ."

"We're having trouble with our oven," Cleo finished.

"Ah," Livy said. "So you're here to speak to Ella."

"Yes," Cleo said. "I suppose we are."

Just then, Ella pushed between her two mothers. Now she was in the doorway, too, right in the center of the group. Where she belonged.

"What have you tried?" she asked.

"We tested the knobs," Leo said.

"How many times?" Ella asked.

"Four," Cleo said.

Ella nodded.

"We tightened everything that could possibly need tightening," Cleo said.

"With what?" Ella asked.

"A wrench," Cleo said.

Ella nodded again.

"We took a carbon monoxide reading."

"And?"

"Perfectly normal," Leo said.

Ella nodded for a third time. "I see," she said. "You thought of everything, and all your thoughts were wrong."

"Well, not *all*—" Leo began.

But Ella raised her hand to stop him. "You're out of ideas, so you've come to me," she said.

"Well—" said Cleo.

"Yes," Leo said.

"I hope you didn't find us rude earlier," Cleo said. "It was just that we had so much to do."

Ella shrugged.

"And now look at us," Leo said. "Here in your doorway, asking you for help."

"Well," Ella said. "Better late than never. Let the tour begin! Mom and Mom, I'll be back in about an hour."

"The tour?" Cleo asked.

"An *hour*!?" Leo said.

"Just the oven is all we need for tonight," Cleo said. "Tour tomorrow, maybe?"

But the door to Apartment C was already shut, and Ella was leading them up the stairs instead of back down them.

CHAPTER FIVE

Ella placed a finger in front of her lips and led Cleo and Leo to the top of the stairs.

"We have to whisper up here."

Cleo's eyes widened.

"Why?" Leo whispered back.

"This is where the Robinsons live. Gertrude and Archibald Robinson. They are ancient. They are sneaky.

I've lived here all my life, but they've lived here for *ages*."

"Ages." Leo nodded. "I understand."

"I recommend that you *never* come up here," Ella said. "Never. Ever."

Cleo whispered, "Can we go back down now?"

"Good idea," Ella said. "Follow me."

She tiptoed down the stairs. Cleo and Leo tiptoed after her. Once they reached the landing, the three of them walked normally again.

"As you know, this is my door," Ella said. "Come by anytime except Fridays from seven to nine, family movie night. We alternate who picks the movie. Just the three of us. But other than that, our door is always open. Or, you know, open*able*."

"That's very generous," Leo said.

"Thank you," said Cleo.

"Sure," Ella said. She crossed the landing to Apartment B.

"Woof!" she called.

Woof, woof! Woof, woof! came from the other side.

"I'd knock, but only the dogs are home this early. Jacques and Merland will be home in around an hour at the earliest. They both work downtown, and they're very social. The dog-sitter always drops the dogs off at six, though. Come on!"

Ella skipped down the next flight of stairs. She put her face right up against the door of Apartment D. "It is I, Empress of 1106 Wildflower Place! Open immediately, I command you!" she thundered.

Then she took a step back to wait.

The door swung open.

"Darling," said a woman in purple pants with long red hair.

"Darling," Ella said back.

They gave each other air kisses as Cleo and Leo watched in astonishment.

"I'm here to introduce the new neighbors," Ella said.

"The neighbors! Of course! I could feel a certain buzz of newness in the air. I could hear the sound of fresh beginnings, of new starts, of settling in!"

"Okay," Ella said. "Or maybe you felt a breeze from the door being propped open, and you heard the sound of the moving truck."

"Sure, whatever. That too."

"Cleo and Leo, meet Matilda."

"You rhyme!" Matilda said. "How delightful."

"We don't have time to come in right now, but we'll have a good visit soon," Ella said.

"Sure, petunia. But hold on just a sec. I have something for you."

Matilda disappeared.

"Don't worry," Ella said. "I factored this waiting time into our hour." She tapped her foot. She sighed. "Matilda's primary hobby is giving me gifts," she explained.

"Okay," Matilda said, reappearing with something complicated and colorful in her hands. "I found this at an art show last week. All this wild performance stuff, totally bonkers, but *here*. Look."

Matilda took hold of a bright blue piece of wood between her two fingers. Slowly, she lifted it up. The rest fell into place. A hill. Clouds. The sun.

"It's a mobile," Matilda said. "You can hang it in your room."

"It's astonishingly beautiful," Ella said, and she meant it. She only ever said what she meant.

"Well," Matilda said. "I'm glad you think so."

"I'm giving the tour, so keep it for now, okay? I'll stop in for tea tomorrow."

Matilda nodded. "See you later, Ella. And see you later, too, Cleo and Leo, my rhyming friends."

CHAPTER SIX

The garden was nestled behind the building. And because Poppy Hill was so very steep, the garden was arranged beside a set of stairs that cut into the hillside. And because 1106 Wildflower Place contained exactly five apartments, the garden was divided into exactly five plots of dirt.

"Do you notice that some of the plots are full of living plants, and others are full of dead ones?" Ella asked.

She was standing at the top of the garden steps, looking down at Cleo and Leo.

"I do," Leo said, and Cleo nodded.

Ella said, "The plots are arranged just like the house, so yours is bottom row, left side."

"The brown, sort of crunchy one?" Leo asked.

"Yes."

"The one with the dried-up weeds and the broken pot?" Cleo asked.

"Afraid so," Ella said. "The one right above yours is ours."

"Wow," said Cleo. "Look at your tomatoes."

"And your corn and your basil."

"Also, peppers and eggplant and a million types of herbs," Ella said. "And the one next to yours is Matilda's. All she grows is flowers. Sometimes, we trade. Jacques and Merland have some kale going, as you can see. They are sometimes-gardeners. They aren't totally devoted."

"And at the top," Cleo said. "Are those . . . *roses* in the Robinsons' plot?"

"Yes," Ella said. "It's a mystery."

Leo furrowed his brow. "I don't see what's so mysterious about some rosebushes."

"Do you see how many blossoms there are?" Ella asked. Cleo and Leo nodded. "Roses aren't easy flowers. They need a lot of tending. The perfect amount of water. Special plant food. Some pruning here and there and plenty of sun and room to grow. They need *attention*. And that's the mystery: We've never *once* seen the Robinsons in the garden."

"Never?" Leo asked.

Ella nodded. "*Ever*. And believe me, I watch for them."

Just then, there was a movement from up above.

A movement from the top floor of 1106 Wildflower Place.

A movement from Apartment A, residence of Gertrude and Archibald Robinson.

Ella, Cleo, and Leo all looked up at the topmost window of the pink building. The curtain was drawn. Strange, since the sun hadn't set yet. Strange, that they would see movement and now only stillness.

Cleo sighed. "Look at this building," she said.

By which she meant *Look at the pink and the green and the gold. Look at the trim with its swirls and stars.*

"It's really something," Leo said.

He put his arm around her. He gazed into her eyes.

Ella cleared her throat.

"It certainly is," Ella agreed. "But it's time to go over the garden rules. Rule one: Organic dirt only. Rule two: You may garden only inside your own plot. Rule three: Garden parties are encouraged, but only after written notification is given to the other tenants at least twenty-four hours in advance."

33

"Okay," Leo said. "Sounds reasonable."

But Cleo tilted her head. "I don't know about that last one. What if we're feeling spontaneous?"

"Resist the feeling," Ella said.

"Why?" Cleo asked.

"Well, it has to do with the person who created the rules, if you know what I mean."

"And that person is . . . ?"

"My mother."

"Which one?" Leo asked.

"Abby," Ella said. "Obviously."

"Why is it obvious?" Cleo asked.

"Livy doesn't believe in rules."

"Hmm," Leo said. "Even for the garden?"

Ella threw her head back and laughed.

She stopped laughing but then started again.

Ella laughed and laughed and laughed while her new neighbors stared at her with matching expressions of concern.

And then she said, "Livy doesn't believe in rules— except for the rules that Abby makes. Those, she has no choice but to follow. Relationships require compromise, you know."

Leo took Cleo's hand and smiled.

"You both are very young," Ella said. "But you'll learn."

CHAPTER SEVEN

The hour had passed. The tour was done. And now they were back in the entry hall, at the foot of the stairs, between the doors to Apartments D and E.

"So that's it," Ella said. "That's the tour. Have a good night!" She turned to the stairs.

"Wait!" Leo said.

Ella turned back around. "Wait for what?"

"Um . . . ," Leo said.

"It's just . . . ," Cleo said.

Ella stared at them. *"What?"*

"Well, weren't you going to . . . ," Leo began.

"We were under the impression that . . . ," Cleo continued.

Ella tapped her foot. "I'm listening," she said.

"The oven?" Cleo asked.

"Of course, the oven!" Ella laughed. "Why didn't you say so?"

She opened the door to Apartment E and led them inside. "All we need is a matchbook," she said, and held out her hand.

"Oh, dear," Cleo said.

They didn't have a matchbook. Ella threw up her hands. She crossed the hallway. Pressed her face against the door.

"It is I, Empress of 1106 Wildflower Place! Open immediately, I command you!"

The door swung open. *"Darling!"* Matilda said.

"Darling!" Ella said. "I need a source of fire, please."

"Sure, one sec."

Matilda appeared with a box of matches.

"Thank you from the bottom of my heart," Ella said.

"You're welcome from the bottom of mine," Matilda said. And then she closed the door.

Ella strode into the kitchen of Apartment E, matches in hand, and stopped in front of the stove. Cleo stood to her right. Leo stood to her left.

"The best way to learn is by doing," Ella said. She handed Cleo the matchbook. "It's a very old oven, so you'll need a big box of matches. Leo, please turn the knob to start the oven. Good. Now open the oven door. Excellent."

Leo smiled, clearly proud of himself.

"Cleo, please light a match," Ella said. "Very nice. Now reach partway into the oven, to where that little piece sticks out."

Cleo did as she was told. There was a faint *swoosh*, followed by a tiny orange flame.

"Now blow out the match. And that," Ella said, "is how you light your oven. What are you cooking?"

"Frozen pizza," Cleo said.

"Frozen pizza," Ella repeated.

It was a rather boring choice for the first night at a residence as exceptional as 1106 Wildflower Place, but Ella tried her best to be nice about it. She shrugged. "Bon appétit," she said.

Just then sounded a tremendous noise.

CHAPTER EIGHT

The noise was deep and low and loud and grand.

"The earth is quaking!" Leo cried.

Cleo and Leo leapt into each other's arms, but Ella barely flinched.

The noise sounded again—deeper and lower and louder and grander than before.

Cleo and Leo held each other closer.

Ella lifted a finger. "One more," she said. "And then it will be over."

BOOOOOM-MMMMSHHHH-BOOOMSHHBOOM  went the sound once more, like Ella said.

And then, like Ella said, it was over.

Cleo and Leo let go of each other.

"What *was* that?" Cleo asked.

"Oh, the sound?" Ella said.

"It wasn't an earthquake, was it?" Leo asked.

"Not at all," Ella said. "I mentioned it this morning, but you weren't paying attention. It's Matilda's giant instrument. It's so rare it doesn't have a name. It fills her entire second bedroom. She bangs it at this time each night. Don't ask me why."

Ella's work here was done for the evening. Of that, she was sure. And so she headed out of Apartment E. She paused in the doorway.

"Welcome to 1106 Wildflower Place," she said.

Cleo smiled. Leo smiled.

"Thank you," they said.

"Come up if you have questions. Any time at all. Well, not on Fridays—"

"From seven to nine," Leo said.

"Movie night," Cleo said.

Ella nodded. "See you soon," she said. "Until then, I'll be on top of your heads."

CHAPTER NINE

After she watered her houseplants and put on her pajamas, brushed her teeth and hair and wrote a top-secret letter, Ella found her parents in the living-room-slash-dining-room-slash-painting-room-slash-office. They were sitting next to each other on the sofa. Abby was reading a magazine while Livy stared quizzically across the room at the painting she'd spent the day working on.

"The new neighbors are okay after all," Ella said.

"I'm glad to hear that," Livy said.

Abby turned the page of her magazine. "I'll be in soon to tuck you in," she said.

"I'm nine," Ella said. "I can tuck myself in, thank you very much."

"I know you can," Abby said. "But do you *want* to?"

Ella thought about it. "No," she said.

Abby nodded and turned another page.

Ella climbed onto her bed and burrowed in. From her bedroom window, the view was perfect.

The up-close roofs of other houses, the tippy-tops of trees. The skyscrapers in the distance. And, above it all, a bright white sliver of moon, hanging gently in the sky.

Ella thought about Cleo and Leo. She thought about Matilda's mermaid hair and Jacques and Merland's happy dogs. She thought of the glimpse of movement from Apartment A and the Robinsons' roses, which were truly magnificent. She thought of her secret letter, full of secret information.

And then came the quiet creak of her bedroom door. The footsteps she knew by heart.

Abby bent over and kissed Ella on the forehead, just as she'd been doing since Ella was born and for nine entire years between then and now.

And then the lights went out, and all was quiet in the second bedroom of 1106 Wildflower Place, Apartment C.

Tea at
Ten O'Clock

CHAPTER ONE

"Where are you going?" Abby asked Ella on Saturday morning.

It was, as always, a bright, sunny day on Poppy Hill. The birds chirped outside and the breeze was just strong enough to carry the scent of the Robinsons' roses up from the garden and through the open windows of Apartment C.

Ella was wearing her nicest pants and had slipped on her nicest shoes.

Abby was wearing her chore clothes and was pulling on her gardening gloves.

"It's ten o'clock," Ella told her mother. "I'm having tea with Matilda."

"But we're gardening together at ten o'clock," said Abby. "See? It's on the calendar."

Ella crossed to the wall where the calendar hung. There it was, clear as every day on Poppy Hill: 10–11 A.M. ABBY & ELLA, GARDEN CHORES.

Ella laughed. "What was I thinking?"

Abby laughed too. "I have no idea!"

"Just a sec," Ella said, heading out the door and down the stairs. She stopped in front of Apartment D.

"It is I, Empress of 1106 Wildflower Place! Open immediately, I command you!" she thundered.

The door swung open. *"Darling!"* Matilda said, holding a bright yellow teapot.

"Darling!" Ella said back. "I must change our plans. I completely overlooked the calendar, and I have chores. See you a little later?"

"Marvelous!" Matilda said, and shut the door.

CHAPTER TWO

Ella and Abby spent an hour in the sun, clearing their plot of weeds and popping tiny orange tomatoes into their mouths. Ella knew that Abby loved dirt in her hands and seeing things grow. Loved pointing to the birds of Poppy Hill and calling them each by their scientific names. And *Ella* loved how relaxed her mom was when she was outdoors. How it felt to work alongside her for each of those sixty minutes.

And now the plot was free of weeds and Ella was all cleaned up from gardening, back in her nicest pants and shoes. For an extra touch, she chose the nicest hat from her collection and placed it at an unusual angle on her head.

"I'm off to Matilda's," she called from the door.

"Wait!" Livy called back. "I need you!"

"For what?" Ella called.

"For *art*!" Livy said.

Ella took a deep breath. Sometimes, when Livy talked about art, Ella had to muster extra patience. She walked into the living-room-slash-dining-room-slash-painting-room-slash-office.

"What *about* art, exactly?" Ella asked.

"Oh, good," Livy said. "You heard me." She was smiling. Her eyes were wide and dreamy. Her fingers fluttered as though she were playing a piano.

"Uh-oh," Ella said.

"I know," Livy said. "Isn't it wonderful?"

"Hold on," Ella said. "I'll be right back."

Ella again stood in front of the door to Apartment D. "It is I, Empress of 1106 Wildflower Place! Open immediately, I command you!"

The door swung open. *"Darling,"* Matilda said. "What a brilliant hat!"

"Livy has been visited by the muse."

"Fantastic!"

"She says she needs my help. Tea in the afternoon?"

"Afternoon tea is divine!"

Back upstairs, Ella took off her hat.

Livy explained what she needed Ella to do.

"Hold this peach. Can you believe how beautiful it is? Toss it up and down in the air a few times. When I tell you to—and not a *moment* sooner—take a bite."

Ella felt herself losing patience. She breathed in and out four times. "Okay," she said.

Livy nodded and locked eyes with her as if they were in on a secret. She stepped behind her canvas and dipped her brush in paint.

"I'm ready," Livy said. "Admire the peach!"

Ella looked at the peach. She examined it. It *was* beautiful. Furry and yellow and light orange and pink. The peach was a little round sunset in her palm. A fragrant, fuzzy sunset.

"Don't bite!" Livy shouted.

Ella jumped. She hadn't even realized that she'd lifted the peach close to her mouth. She looked at the clock.

"Toss it around now," Livy said. Ella tossed the peach, and Livy dipped more brushes into her paints.

After a while, Ella said, "I should start eating the peach now. Time is passing."

"What *is* time, even?" Livy exclaimed. "We have lives to live! Art to lose ourselves in! I say we throw away the clocks!"

Abby stood near them at the table, the family calendar laid out in front of her. She was filling in the month of October, even though it was only July.

"Time is how society functions," Abby said without looking up. "Time holds everything together."

"Ugh!" Ella said. "I'm eating the peach now."

CHAPTER THREE

Ella ate her peach along with a sandwich. She washed her dishes and her hands when she was finished. In her room, she put on her nicest hat—*again*. When she opened her door, Abby was there, holding out the phone.

"It's Jacques," she said. "Calling for you."

Ella threw up her hands. *What now?*

"Ella, thank goodness you're home," Jacques said. "The dog walker quit!"

"Well, that's a problem," Ella said. "But you can rely on me. One walk now and another after dinner."

"Do you still have your key?"

"Of course."

"What on *earth* would we do without you, Ella?"

"I honestly don't know," Ella said.

On a shelf by her bedroom window was a wooden box. Inside the box were the spare keys to Apartments B, D, and E. Ella took out the key to Apartment B and closed the lid.

She ran downstairs. *"Another problem!"* she called through the door. *"I'll be back in a little while!"*

"Whenever!" Matilda called from somewhere inside Apartment D.

Ella let herself into Jacques and Merland's apartment.

"Hi, Daisy," she said to the tiny poodle.

"Hi, Danny," she said to the golden retriever.

Unlike her family's living room, this one wasn't trying to be too many things. It had a sofa and a dog bed, a bookshelf and a TV. On the bookshelf sat a framed picture of Jacques and Merland's wedding day, with Ella in the center of it.

Jacques's niece was supposed to be the flower girl, but she got food poisoning the night before, and Ella had been there to save the day, as she always did.

Ella smiled at herself in the photo, two years younger and holding a gigantic bouquet of magnificent roses, standing between Jacques and Merland, each of them with perfect smiles of their own.

On each side of the happy couple was a dog.

The dogs were next to Ella now, gazing along with her at the photograph.

"It was a good day," she said to them. "It was a very happy day, wasn't it?"

Daisy yelped. Danny wagged his tail. She patted Danny on the head and bent down to pat Daisy, too. Ella cared about fairness. She would never deny Daisy a head pat, even if the little dog's head was ridiculously close to the floor.

"All right, you two. I have plans. Tea in Apartment D with Matilda. So let's go ahead and take our walk, and then I will continue with my day."

Daisy did a funny little dance, not unlike chasing her own tail. Danny rubbed his head against Ella's side. Ella took the leashes from the basket by the door.

"Okay, pups," she said. "Let's go."

CHAPTER FOUR

Just as Ella reached the bottom of the stairs, Daisy and Danny by her side, the door to Apartment E swung open.

"Ella!" Cleo said.

"Ella!" Leo said.

"Hello," said Ella.

"We're *so* glad we caught you," Cleo said.

Ella waited.

"Are you having a good day?" Leo asked.

Ella shrugged. Matilda's door was so close. Ella was so ready for tea. Time was passing with every moment.

"Do you need something?" Ella asked.

"Well, you know . . . ," Leo said.

"No," said Ella. "I don't."

"We were wondering . . . ," Cleo said.

"About what?"

"Didn't you mention something about . . . ," Leo began.

"A light switch?" Cleo asked. "A . . . *glitch?*"

Ella threw up her hands. "Why didn't you say so?!" She turned to the dogs. "Daisy. Danny. I'll be right back." The dogs sat.

Ella led Cleo and Leo into Apartment E. She crossed to the hallway.

"Observe," she said. She turned the light switch

on. It did nothing. She jiggled it up and down several times. "Now count to three," she said.

Cleo and Leo counted.

"Now stomp," Ella said.

Cleo and Leo stomped.

The light turned on.

"Practice a few times," Ella said. "You'll get the hang of it."

CHAPTER FIVE

Ella fastened Daisy's purple leash and Danny's pink one.
She took a deep breath and let it out. This day was not
going according to plan, but she'd try to make the best
of it. Daisy and Danny led her down the front steps and
to the left, toward the dog park.

Sometimes, when Ella walked she became con-
templative. Sometimes, she asked herself big questions
about life.

Today, she thought about days. How an entire day could pass while she read a book in her mint-green chair, only stopping for snacks and bathroom breaks. How another could be full of chores and errands and saving various people in a variety of ways. How some days seemed to move as slowly as a snail across her family's garden plot, while others darted past like hummingbirds.

Was time something to let go of, like Livy thought? Or was Abby right? Did time hold everything together?

Ella took the leashes off the dogs and let them run around in the park. They leapt and wrestled, yipped and howled.

Do dogs ever think about time? she wondered.

When they returned to their block, before climbing the stairs, Ella took a moment to admire the apartment house. It was so beautifully grand and pink. Its trim was so enchantingly green and gold and swirly. Its roof was so perfectly pointy.

She unlocked the door to the entry hall and froze. She could have sworn she'd seen a blur of motion between the mailboxes and the stairs, but now all was still.

She took Daisy and Danny back up to Apartment B. She filled their bowls with kibble. She patted them on their heads.

"Be good," she told them, and then she went downstairs alone.

CHAPTER SIX

"It is I . . . ," Ella began. And then she just opened the door.

"Darling," Matilda said.

"I'm here," Ella said.

The apartment was quiet. The sun shone through the bank of windows at the perfect angle, and Ella threw herself across a soft blanket, atop a soft pillow, atop a stack of soft, soft rugs.

"You must be warm from your walk," Matilda said, appearing with a giant fan made of ostrich feathers.

Ella closed her eyes.

She felt the softness and the breeziness.

She let out a long sigh.

When the fanning was over and the tea was ready, Ella sat up.

"What is your philosophy of time?" she asked.

"Hmm," Matilda said. "I don't know if I have one. But I like to think of us on our strange little planet, spinning in the vastness of the solar system."

Ella nodded. "Tell me more," she said. "Tell me anything you want to say about time."

"Well, I wake up very early for work. Did you know that?"

"How early?"

"Five o'clock! I like to be up before it's light. It feels like a secret between me and the day."

Ella sipped her tea, sweetened with honey.

"And when I pour hot water over tea leaves," Matilda said, "I always wait for precisely three minutes to let it steep."

"How do you know it's precisely three minutes?"

"I'll show you."

Matilda went to the kitchen and returned with a tiny hourglass.

"Are you ready?" she asked.

Ella nodded.

Matilda turned the hourglass over so that all the sand was on top and set it on the coffee table between them. The sand began to slip through the narrow center. Ella and Matilda watched.

Slowly, steadily, the sand fell.

They sat still.

The apartment was quiet.

Three full minutes went by. The last speck of sand slipped through.

Ella smiled. Matilda smiled.

"Oh," Matilda said. "Well, look at that. Night is falling already. Will you excuse me for a moment?"

"Of course," Ella said. She lay back on the pillow and closed her eyes and waited.

Boomshhh, she heard from the second bedroom, so loud she felt a tremor.

Booomshhhh, she heard again, and the teacups clattered in their saucers.

BOOOOOMMMMMSHHHHBOOOMSHH-BOOM, went the third and final strike of Matilda's gigantic instrument.

And then it was over, and Ella stood up as Matilda came back to the room. They carried their cups and saucers to the kitchen sink. Matilda set her hourglass on the windowsill.

"Good night, darling," Ella said. "Thanks for the tea."

"Anytime," Matilda said. "Oh, don't forget your hat."

And the earth spun.

And the sky darkened.

And the stars shone.

And time passed, in one way or another.

The
Greatest Mystery
of All Time

CHAPTER ONE

It was a sunny afternoon on Poppy Hill, as all afternoons on Poppy Hill were. Ella had finished her chores and read her book, which meant it was time for her to go to the garden to see if a secret letter awaited her.

Down she went. Outside she went. To the garden she went.

There was an envelope, under a rock.

She smiled. She opened it.

Dear Ella, she read. *We have found ourselves in need of a favor. Please come see us in Apartment A at your earliest convenience. Best regards, Gertrude and Archibald Robinson. PS: By your earliest convenience, we mean now.*

Ella's eyes widened, and her breath caught, and she felt as though her *whole* life—the entire nine years, two months, three days, and seven hours of it—had been spent in preparation for what she was about to do.

Her hands trembled in wonder.

Her heart thudded in excitement.

So much had happened to lead her to this moment.

So very, very much.

CHAPTER TWO

Sometimes, a moment is more than a moment. Sometimes, a moment holds so much meaning it's difficult to
make sense of it all. In order to understand it, Ella knew,
she would need to let her thoughts travel back in time.

It began when she came to live at 1106 Wildflower
Place, Apartment C, when she was one day old. Like all
babies, at first she was unaware of the world. All she

knew was when she was hungry and when she was full. When she was content and when she was not.

Soon, she recognized voices.

And textures and colors and shapes.

She learned the words *flower* and *sun*.

And the words *stairs* and *doors* and *neighbors* and *apartment house*.

And with those words, her life blossomed into something very interesting.

"Who is *upstairs?*" she asked her mothers when she was three.

"Gertrude and Archibald Robinson," Livy said.

"Who are *they?*"

Abby and Livy looked at each other. Livy shrugged.

Abby said, "Well, sweetie pie, I guess no one really knows."

It isn't easy for a girl who knows nearly everything about a place to know absolutely nothing about one piece of it, and that's what life was like for Ella for a very long time.

The other apartments each shared a floor, and their layouts were identical. At dinnertime, the residents of Apartment C stood at their stove right above where the residents of Apartment E stood at theirs. The same went for Jacques and Merland, who stood right above Matilda. The water from their sinks poured into the same pipes.

But Apartment A had the top floor to itself. No way to know where the stove was or even the kitchen, for that matter. Apartment A had windows all over the place. Apartment A's ceilings were most certainly not flat like the ceilings were in Apartments B through E, because Apartment A was right under the slanted, perfectly pointy roof with its eaves and its tower.

In other words, Apartment A was the crown jewel of 1106 Wildflower Place.

And it was the only part of the building that Ella had never been invited into.

For years and years, Ella would exclaim to her mothers and her neighbors and her friends and her teachers, to casual acquaintances and pets and even houseplants, "*What* kind of people keep completely to themselves? Who on *earth* would live on top of my head for my *entire* life and never *once* say hello?"

She spent hours and hours sitting very, very still— a difficult thing for a girl like Ella to do—waiting to hear them above her.

She listened for footsteps. For voices. For laughter or shouting.

She listened for the ring of a phone or the shrill of a teakettle.

She listened for a television or a radio or a toilet flushing.

Nothing.

It seemed impossible that anyone lived in Apartment A at all, but Ella and her neighbors knew for sure that they did.

The Robinsons' mail arrived each day along with everyone else's, and each day—*somehow*—the mail was collected.

Everyone shared the laundry machines down in the basement. Abby had made little signs for each of the residents to set on top of the machines when in use. The ROBINSONS sign was set out as frequently as any of the others were, but no one had ever seen the residents of Apartment A in the basement.

Once, when Ella had seen the Robinsons' sign set out on the dryer, Ella had brought a garden chair into the basement along with a book. She was determined to stay there all day and night if she needed to.

Surely, this way, she would finally meet Gertrude or Archibald.

But by late afternoon she was desperate for a bathroom break, and in the three minutes it took her to rush up to Apartment C and back down again, the Robinsons had snatched their clothes from the dryer. They'd even returned their sign to the shelf!

And then, of course, there were the roses. Six magnificent bushes that burst with color from the Robinsons' garden plot. Each bush was a different type of rose, their flower petals variously shaped, their colors ranging from bright red to peach to purple to pink, their fragrances one of a kind.

All the residents of 1106 Wildflower Place loved the roses, each in their own way.

"These roses could win prizes," Abby said.

"When I'm sad," Jacques said, "I go outside to smell the purple ones. They always make me feel better."

Merland liked the peach ones best. "They remind me of my mother," he said.

Matilda often spread her picnic blanket alongside the bushes, closed her eyes, and breathed in their scent.

Livy admired each flower up close until her eyes got dreamy, her fingers fluttered, and she rushed back in to paint.

"Maybe we'll grow roses like this when we're old," Leo said, taking Cleo's hand.

"Yes," Cleo told him. "Maybe we will."

To be quite honest, when Ella was younger, she wanted to *not* like the roses. She was angry with Gertrude and Archibald. She resented their reclusiveness.

But that was before Jacques and Merland's wedding day.

Because on that day—*exactly* two years ago, in fact—when Ella was seven years old and the residents of Apartment B exchanged vows, everything that Ella believed about the Robinsons changed.

CHAPTER THREE

The morning of Jacques and Merland's wedding was, as always, a beautiful morning on Poppy Hill.

But it was also a disaster.

First, Jacques woke to a call from his sister with news that his niece had gotten food poisoning and would be unable to fulfill her duties as flower girl. Luckily, Ella was available to step in. Abby rushed her to Poppy Street's best clothing store to find a fancy-enough dress while Livy made a garland of wildflowers and ribbons for Ella to wear on her head.

The wedding was to be in the garden of 1106 Wildflower Place (why go elsewhere when your own home was so perfect?), and Ella practiced walking down the garden steps, tossing imaginary flower petals from her basket.

"Lovely!" Merland said. "And just *wait* until the actual flower petals arrive!"

But right then Merland's phone rang. The flower petals would not be arriving. Nor would the actual flowers. No boutonnieres for the grooms. No bouquets for the tables. The flower truck had gotten a flat tire and could not make it in time.

"It's okay," Jacques said, acting brave. "Look at this beautiful garden. Look at this beautiful day. Who needs flowers?"

But everyone needs flowers, especially on their wedding day.

Ella looked at the Robinsons' rosebushes, all six of them in full bloom. *If only* . . . , she thought.

And then came a flutter from the tippy-top window. And, to Ella's astonishment, she thought she saw two faces peering out.

Ella blinked.

The curtain was closed.

How very strange, Ella thought.

Jacques and Merland returned to Apartment B. Ella and her mothers returned to Apartment C. In her room, Ella wrote a note.

She folded it three times, pulled a gold star off her favorite sheet of stickers, and sealed it shut. She dashed out the door and up the stairs to Apartment A. She took a deep breath. She knocked. She heard the faintest and softest of sounds. The *pat-pat* of slippered feet on a plush rug, maybe. She hoped so.

She pushed the note halfway under the door.

She watched as the other half disappeared.

CHAPTER FOUR

Seven-year-old Ella changed into her flower girl dress. It was a little frilly for her taste, and a bit itchy, but today was not a day for complaining. She let Livy place the garland on her head and pin it to her hair. One of the pins poked her, but she didn't even flinch. It was not a day for flinching. She let Abby button her buttons and straighten her hem—as though she were a baby! But she wouldn't protest. No. This was Jacques and Merland's day. Cooperating was the least she could do.

"Ready?" Abby asked.

"Ready," Ella said.

Livy said, "You look beautiful."

Ella said thank you.

The three of them opened their door. The three of them gasped.

All across the landing between Apartments B and C were roses. Roses in vases for the tables. Roses bound in ribbon for the tuxes. Rose petals in a basket for Ella to carry. There were even tiny rosebuds meant for Daisy's and Danny's collars.

"Jacques! Merland!" Abby called. "It's a miracle!"

But Ella only smiled.

It wasn't a miracle.

It was the Robinsons.

And, well, it was a little bit *Ella*, too.

The garden was crammed with happy guests, and no one but Ella seemed to notice that the Robinsons' rosebushes, just an hour ago bursting with flowers, were now almost bare.

The ceremony began. Ella walked down the steps, scattered the rose petals, and took her seat between Livy and Abby.

A few minutes later, Ella thought she felt someone watching from above. She turned. There they were, the curtain drawn, the window flung open.

Gertrude and Archibald Robinson, their wise old cheeks pressed together, smiles on each of their faces, watching Jacques and Merland say "I do."

Dear Gertrude and Archibald, Ella had written on a card that night after the reception was over. *Thank you for the flowers. I would like to meet you someday, if that's something you would like, too. Love, Ella Josephine Norwood, Apartment C.*

She left the note under a rock in their garden plot the next morning.

Dear Gertrude and Archibald,

Thank you for the flowers. I would like to meet you someday, if that's something you would like, too.

Love,
Ella Josephine Norwood
Apartment C

The afternoon after that, she found a different note, left in the same place.

Dear Ella, We are very shy, but we know who you are. We couldn't imagine a better girl to live right beneath our kitchen. Love, Archibald and Gertrude Robinson.

Dear Ella,

We are very shy, but we know who you are. We couldn't imagine a better girl to live right beneath our kitchen.

Love,
Archibald and Gertrude Robinson
X

Their kitchen! One tiny part of the mystery revealed.

And from that day forward, Ella knew that the Robinsons—however shy they were, however sneaky—were very good neighbors indeed.

CHAPTER FIVE

Nine-year-old Ella was now standing in the garden, holding a note.

She looked up to the tippy-top window and saw nothing at first. And then she saw the curtain flutter, the window inch open, and a very old hand stick out and wave.

"I'll be right there," Ella called.

She stopped at Apartment C on her way up. Her parents were putting a puzzle together at the table in the living-room-slash-dining-room-slash-painting-room-slash-office.

"I need to tell you something," Ella said. Neither of her parents looked up. "For the last two years, I've been leaving notes for the Robinsons in their garden plot."

"Yes," Abby said, picking up a puzzle piece. "We know."

This took Ella by surprise, but she continued. "For the last two years, the Robinsons have been writing back."

"Yes," Livy said. "We know that, too."

"Ugh!" Ella said. "Well anyway. Now they need a favor. They've invited me upstairs."

Abby and Livy looked up from the puzzle.

"Oh!" Livy said.

"Wow!" Abby said.

Abby and Livy smiled at Ella. Ella smiled back.

Ella climbed the stairs to Apartment A.

She'd climbed the stairs many times before. She'd even sat on the landing, holding an empty water glass to the door, hoping it would help her hear the goings-on inside.

But this time felt different. She slowed as she reached the landing. Her life was about to change—she knew it. And then she was in front of the door. She lifted her hand to knock, but she didn't need to.

The knob turned silently.

The door opened without even the slightest creak or groan.

"Come in," a kind voice whispered.

It was the voice of Gertrude Robinson.

"It's such a pleasure to meet you," said Archibald.

"It's a pleasure to . . . ," Ella began, but she couldn't find the words to continue. Because there in front of her were the people she'd seen from the window, the people she was prepared to meet.

But she was not prepared for what was behind them.

CHAPTER SIX

Ella stepped into the apartment in a daze. She didn't ask for a tour, but Gertrude and Archibald beamed with pride as Ella explored the rooms. Wallpaper with giant burgundy roses—roses as big as her head!—covered the walls. The chandeliers were shaped like roses. The sofa was rose-patterned, with rose-printed pillows heaped on top. The dining table was covered in a rose table-cloth, with painted rose china and rose-etched glasses set for two. In the table's center were tiny salt-and-pepper shakers. Roses, both.

The hallway was lined with framed photographs. Some were of people or places. Most were of roses.

The bathroom was wallpapered in a different pattern—white wild roses with some yellow ones, too. Rose-scented soap rested in a rose-shaped dish by the sink.

The kitchen had roses carved into the cabinets and paintings of roses on the wall by the stove and a bouquet of cut roses, fresh from the garden.

Ella felt a bit dizzy. She'd spent so many years wondering and dreaming and wishing for a glimpse of the Robinsons and a visit to Apartment A. And now here she was—and here *they* were—and it was . . .

"Spectacular," she said.

Gertrude squeezed her hands together in pleasure. Archibald's wide smile grew even wider.

"You said you needed a favor?" Ella asked, remembering.

"Oh, we do, dear," Archibald said.

"Here." Gertrude beckoned her into the dining room. "Let me show you."

On the sideboard rested a tangle of ribbon.

"We need to tie some bows," Gertrude said. "But it's all in a knot."

"We've tried and tried," Archibald said. "But look at these fingers! We aren't quite as nimble as we used to be."

The Robinsons showed Ella their hands. Swollen knuckles and calloused fingertips. Who knew how many rosebushes those hands had tended? Ella looked at her own hands. They were slender and small.

"I'd be happy to help," she said.

She perched on a rose-colored chair in the living room, across from the Robinsons, who sat on their sofa.

"Would you like some rose-petal tea?" Gertrude asked.

"Of course," Ella replied.

The ribbon was white with pink roses on it and tangled in many places. But little by little, the knots came undone. And Ella's attention was now fixed on a curious assortment of objects on the coffee table.

"What are these for?" she asked.

"They're gifts!" Gertrude said. "I'm sure you've noticed, but there's so much to celebrate under this roof."

"It's Jacques and Merland's wedding anniversary," Ella said. "I *do* know that."

"Yes," Archibald said. "They get a sturdy cotton blanket for their visits to the park. They're always coming home with grass stains on their trousers. And this one is for Matilda." He lifted a bell. "She got promoted at work."

"She did?" Ella asked. "How do you know?"

"Well," Gertrude said, "we were doing our laundry, and the basement window was open. And *Matilda's* window was also open. And we heard Matilda say, 'That's wonderful news! Thank you, Harry. I won't let you down.'"

"And?" Ella said.

"Well, Harry is Matilda's boss, you know," Gertrude said. Ella didn't know, which was confusing, because Ella knew Matilda very well. "Anyway, Matilda likes to mark shifts in the day with sound."

"I'll say," said Ella.

"This," said Archibald, ringing the bell, "is quite a perfect sound for the morning. Not too loud for the five o'clock hour but still satisfying."

"Cleo and Leo downstairs have *lots* to celebrate," Gertrude said. "Moving in, of course. And I saw Cleo's little diamond ring through my binoculars. But if Leo keeps forgetting their dinner on the stove the whole place will burn down. We got them a kitchen timer."

Ella counted the gifts. Two were left.

"One for Abby and one for Livy," Archibald said.

"Your mothers are very different people," Gertrude explained. Ella nodded. This was true. "For Livy, we have this crystal to hang in the window. At certain hours of the day, when the light hits it just so, it will cast little rainbows on the walls."

"Oh!" Ella said. "She's always talking about color and light."

"I thought that might be the case," Gertrude said with a mischievous smile. "For Abby, we've chosen this lovely print."

Archibald unfurled it for Ella to see. It showed the phases of the moon for the entire next year against a midnight-blue background.

"She likes to know what to expect," Archibald said. "And she is very fond of nature."

Ella nodded again. This, also, was true.

She took another look at the gifts. The blanket for Jacques and Merland, the timer for Leo and Cleo, the bell for Matilda, the crystal, and the moons. That was all.

Ella blinked.

When her eyes opened, there, right before her at the edge of the table, sat a small box with a bow.

"Where did that come from?"

Gertrude shrugged one of her shoulders and hummed a little question. Archibald winked.

"For me?" Ella asked.

"Go ahead, dear," Archibald said.

Ella took the box in her hands. She pulled at the edge of the bow, and the ribbon fell open. She lifted the lid. Inside was a small, hard, shiny thing. She took it between her fingers. It was a little gold pin in the shape of a rose.

"Allow me?" Gertrude asked, and Ella nodded.

Ella held her breath while Gertrude fastened the pin to her T-shirt pocket. She noticed that Gertrude's fingers were suspiciously nimble.

Gertrude finished and sat back onto the sofa. The Robinsons watched Ella. She could feel them waiting for something.

"Thank you," Ella said.

The Robinsons waited.

"It's a very lovely pin," Ella added.

Still, the Robinsons waited.

And then Gertrude pulled back the top of her cardigan sweater and pointed to the collar of her rose-patterned blouse. Ella's eyes widened. A matching pin!

Archibald tilted his head to the ceiling. There, on the underside of the brim of his wool hat, was a third pin.

"Is *this* . . . ?" Ella asked. "Am *I* . . . ?"

"Yes," Archibald said.

Gertrude nodded. "You're one of us now. You've always been a rare and precious girl."

"Divine," Archibald said. "And, at times, a little thorny." He smiled and winked.

"And *oh*," Gertrude said, touching her heart. "Oh, how you've blossomed."

CHAPTER SEVEN

They drank their tea and wrapped the gifts.

"So," Ella asked when their jobs were done. "How are you planning to give these out? Or rather, how are *we*?"

"Sneakily," Archibald said with a smile.

"As always," Gertrude added, a sparkle in her eyes.

Ella remembered the shifting of curtains. The blur of motion between the mailbox and the landing. The silence of the upstairs. She remembered the laundry room sign set back on its shelf and the dozens of notes left for her over the last two years, notes she never saw the Robinsons leave, no matter how long or how often she'd peered out her window to look.

She remembered nine *years* of searching and waiting and looking for clues.

She sat up straighter. She glanced at the pin on her pocket. "I'm ready," she said.

"Very good," Archibald said. "Because it's almost time."

Time. It was such a simple word, but it swirled through Ella's mind. The way it made people hurry or wait. How small it could be, like sand falling in an hourglass. How vast it could be, like all the seconds of her life that led up to this one.

Gertrude checked her watch. "In about three minutes, Cleo and Leo will return from work, and Jacques and Merland will be back from their evening dog walk. Matilda will be cooking her dinner. Livy will be closing up her paints, and Abby will have collected her lettuces from the garden."

Ella, who thought she knew everything about the apartment house on Poppy Hill, realized how much she had yet to learn. Her dismay must have shown because Archibald peered at her very kindly through his glasses and said, "We will teach you, dear. We have days and months and years ahead of us."

"And so many tricks," Gertrude said with a grin. "But for now—*Up! Up!* Here we go!"

In a flash, the Robinsons were at their door. Ella hurried through the apartment to keep up, carrying all the boxes.

"Shhhh," Gertrude said, but Ella was quite familiar with tiptoeing across their landing and down to the middle floor. She set Jacques and Merland's gift by their door and her mothers' gifts across the landing.

She and Gertrude hurried toward the first level and then turned to find Archibald sailing down the bannister.

"What a show-off," Gertrude whispered, her eyes especially sparkly.

Ella set down Cleo and Leo's gift, followed by Matilda's.

"Now run upstairs and listen closely," Archibald told Ella. "It's almost time."

Ella slipped into Apartment C so softly that her mothers didn't hear her. She pressed her ear against the door and closed her eyes. She stood very still. She breathed in and breathed out. She heard the first ding of a doorbell, and another, and another, and her own.

She heard faraway voices:

"I'll get it, darling."

"Now who could that be?"

"Daisy, Danny, away from the door!"

—and voices just behind her, too:

"Oh, Ella, you're home! Who's at the door?"

"Tell us everything!"

She heard footsteps. Floorboards creaking, people moving. She felt the press of the rose pin against her heart.

And all at once, the residents of 1106 Wildflower Place opened their doors.

THE END